## *Introduction*

Fairy Camellia is surprised when she is woken up from her sleep in Fairyland only to find out that there is a war starting in her forest. Camellia is almost sure it's the wicked fairy named Muddy, but she still has to discover the reason.

When no one wants to accompany her on her scary and dangerous journey to Swampdirt except two small butterflies, she faces her fears and realizes that determination is the key to success.

The wicked fairy is too evil, but how far can kindness go? Can Camellia win her? Discover with Camellia the most important secret that's more powerful than magic itself.

# Chapter 1. The Journey

The moon was lighting the forest in Fairyland with a dim light. A pretty fairy was flying through the green leaves of the trees, her beautiful transparent blue wings shivering in the light breeze. She was very beautiful, with long brown curly hair that reached her waist, blue eyes that sparkled in the dark and light pink dress that looked like a flower. And it was no wonder that it looked like a flower, because Camellia was the Fairy of Flowers, and she smelled like flowers, too. There were two colorful butterflies on her sides, trying to keep up with her.

"Camellia, please slow down a little bit," one of the butterflies said breathlessly. "I can't fly so fast."

"Why, my dear Pinkie?" Camellia asked, turning round to look at the butterfly. Her voice was sweet and quiet.

"I am tired already," Pinkie answered.

"Yes, me, too," said the other butterfly. "My wings hurt from so much flying."

"Oh, Viol, we have just started our journey, and you are already tired?" Camellia asked, smiling. She slowed down a little. "I just wanted to reach Swampdirt before morning. But if you are really tired, we can take a rest here."

Camellia lowered and sat down under a cherry tree. The butterflies sat down onto the pretty flowers next to Camellia.

"Is Swampdirt far from here?" Pinkie asked.

"Yes, I think," Camellia said. "When the moonlight will start to get through the trees with difficulty and the trees will be dried up, when the green grass will become black soil and the pretty lakes will become swamps, then we will know we have reached Swampdirt."

"That sounds really horrible," Viol said, shuddering. Her light blue wings shivered.

"Viol, my dear, you can still return back to the forest if you don't want to come with us," Camellia said kindly. "I and Pinkie will go without you, of course if Pinkie still wants to come with me on this journey."

"Of course I do!" Pinkie shouted.

"I do, too!" Viol said. "I cannot leave you alone, even though I am a bit scared of that awful Fairy of

Swamps."

"There is nothing to be afraid of," Camellia said. "If we hold together, we will overcome all the obstacles. We just need to be full of determination to overcome our worst enemy – fear."

"I am full of determination!" Pinkie exclaimed.

"Me, too!" Viol said. "That is why I am still here, with you."

"Wonderful," Camellia said, picking up a pretty pink flower and attaching it onto her hair. "Now, if you have rested a bit, we can continue our journey. Do you agree with me my beautiful butterflies?"

"Yes, of course," the butterflies said and flew off the flowers.

Camellia got up, too, and flew together with the butterflies. She looked around as she flew and noticed that the freshness of the trees around her was starting to fade, as the moonlight was getting blocked with clouds more often. She didn't say anything, but she realized that Swampdirt wasn't too far away already.

The moon was being blocked by darker clouds already, and the trees were becoming more and more parched. Soon she couldn't even find a single leaf on the trees and the ground was muddy.

"Camellia!" Pinkie exclaimed. "The trees are dry and there is no moonlight!"

"You are right, Pinkie…"

"Look! Look!" Viol shrieked. "The green grass is gone and the pretty lakes have turned into dirty swamps!"

"Exactly," Camellia said, looking down at the dark ground and the swamps that could frequently be seen here and there.

Just at that moment the pretty pink flower disengaged from her head and started to fall down. There was a big swamp underneath.

"Oh, no! My beautiful flower!" Camellia exclaimed and flew downwards, to get her flower mid-air. But she wasn't fast enough, and the flower landed right onto the swamp. Camellia approached the dirty swamp, on the surface of which lay her flower. She tried to pick it up carefully, while shaking her wings vigorously, but her fingertip touched the swamp surface.

Right in that second her wings stopped working and she fell into the swamp.

"Help me! Pinkie! Viol!" she was shrieking, flailing her arms helplessly.

"Oh, Viol, look!" Pinkie exclaimed from above. "Camellia fell into the swamp!"

"And she doesn't seem to be able to come out!" Viol shrieked.

The two butterflies shot down in their biggest

speed and reached the swamp. Each butterfly held Camellia's one hand and they dragged her upwards, to get her out of the swamp.

"Camellia, why are you so heavy!" Viol was panting, as they got her out of the swamp.

"Oh, no! Look at my feet!" Camellia shrieked, looking down at her feet, while still hanging by her arms in the mid-air.

A big octopus was clinging to her feet with its many tentacles, and smiling upwards at her. Apparently it lived in the swamp and was happy to get out of it sometimes.

"Get off me! Get off me!" Camellia was shouting and shaking her legs, trying to drop the octopus.

The butterflies were barely able to hold her in the air, as she was trying to drop the uninvited guest back into its swamp. At last the octopus loosened its grip on her legs and slumped down into the swamp with a loud cling.

Camellia breathed with relief. But she was worried – she could not fly.

"Pinkie, Viol, please put me onto the ground," she said. "Something is wrong. I can't fly."

The butterflies landed onto the ground and put her onto her feet.

"What has happened, Camellia?" Viol asked, her voice shaking.

Camellia tried to shake her wings, but they were so dirty with swamp mud that they had stuck together and weren't moving. She was overall very dirty, and covered with mud.

"My wings, they are so dirty!" She exclaimed with disgust. "Let me just wash them, all right?"

She clicked her fingers and clapped her hands, rubbed her thumbs with index fingers, trying to create sparkles, like she used to do, but nothing happened.

"I don't understand, what is happening?" she said worriedly. "Why can't I do my magic?"

The butterflies looked at each other, looking alarmed.

Camellia sat down under one of the perched trees, looking puzzled and sad. The butterflies sat down on her sides, not knowing what to say. The fairy that had lost her powers to do her magic could not be considered a fairy anymore.

"But why did I lose my powers the second I touched that swamp?" Camellia wondered out loud.

"Maybe the swamp was full of magic?" Pinkie suggested.

"I also think so," Camellia said. "Muddy, the Fairy of Swamps, may have put a dark spell on the swamps."

"I can't believe she is so evil," Viol whispered.

"Well, I guess she has just taken security measures," Camellia said. "This is her area, remember? We are already in Swampdirt. Too bad that I wasn't cautious enough and touched the swamp."

"She just doesn't want to be invaded by enemies," Pinkie said angrily. "Like she invaded our forest last night!"

Camellia slowly nodded. What had happened the previous night was the reason she had started that journey to Swampdirt.

## Chapter 2. The Previous Night

Camellia remembered everything that had happened to their forest the previous night. And it was awful. Here is what had happened the previous night:

All the fairies were sleeping peacefully in their homes. Camellia was asleep in her beautiful pink flower house, Willay, the Fairy of Trees in her tree house, Reddie, the Fairy of Fire in her flame house, Shampina, the Fairy of Mushrooms in her big mushroom house, Fluffy, the Fairy of Clouds in her little cloud house and many many other fairies in their special houses.

Suddenly they heard the buzzing sound of hundreds of insects, and at the same time the little pretty houses of the fairies started to collapse. The fairies woke up and looked around: the mosquitoes, wasps and dragonflies were flying towards them, glaring at them angrily, while the spiders, scorpions and snakes were crawling on the ground, trying to reach them.

Shrieks filled the forest. It was obvious that the

insects and the snakes had been made magically stronger, otherwise they would not be able to cause all that disruption in the forest. Camellia looked around: in the dark she could hardly see the insects attacking the fairies. It didn't take long for the fairies to fully wake up and start to defend themselves.

Raya, the Fairy of the Sun, started directing sharp sunrays towards the attackers. The wasps quickly changed the direction of their attack, dodging the sunrays. In the meantime, Blowie, the Fairy of the Wind, was blowing cold wind towards them, pushing the dragonflies backwards. The dragonflies struggled, but couldn't fly forward: the strong wind was pushing them back. A little over there Reddie was trying to burn them with fire that she had conjured out of thin air.

Camellia didn't do any magic. She was just looking at the battle in the forest, trying to understand what was going on. She approached Willay, who was busy in the tree trunk, looking for something.

"Willay, why are we fighting with them?" She asked.

"Don't you see it, Camellia?" Willay turned around to look at Camellia, sounding surprised. "We are doing counter-attacks, because they started it first."

"I see it, of course," Camellia said. "But I don't know what the reason of this war is. Maybe we should at first find out the reason?"

"There is no time for finding out reasons,

Camellia," Willay said and turned back to the tree trunk. "A snake has bitten poor Rainbow's leg, and now she can't move. I've got to take some Healing Scrape off this tree – it has healing powers. And hopefully then I will manage to get rid of some of the attackers with my magical wooden stick."

Camellia sighed and turned back to look at the war.

"Ouch, my leg!" Blowie screamed, just as Camellia saw a big black scorpion stinging her. Camellia flew away to the place where special flowers grew. The Poison-Lilies. They were most effective against the scorpions' poison. They grew a bit far from the place that the fairies lived. She could hardly see in the dark, but she knew the exact location of the wonderful flowers. Picking up several of those flowers, Camellia swiftly flew back and put the petals on Blowie's leg.

"Is it better now, Blowie?" She asked. "Just wait a few seconds, and the poison will be entirely gone!"

"Thank you!" Blowie said, smiling with gratitude. "Are you looking for any wounded fairies and healing them? It is also very useful during wars, you know?"

Camellia didn't want the war to take place. She didn't want to rescue fairies, nor did she want to get rid of the insect.

"Stop fighting, please!" She screamed, but no one paid attention to her.

Shampina clicked her fingers and produced green sparkles, which immediately flew towards the small mushrooms, making them poisonous. Then she grabbed them and threw onto the spiders that were drawing closer to her.

"Please don't kill them," Camellia was asking the other fairies.

"Not that it's easy to kill them – they're fast and strong, probably stronger than us," Grassina, the Fairy of Grass told her, brushing a nasty cockroach off her light green dress and clicking her fingers to create magical sparkle.

The night's dark air was full of magical sparkles, razor-sharp sunrays, swirling wind and flaming fire, so it was almost impossible to see anything. The angry wasps and other insects made such a buzzing noise, that it was almost impossible to hear anything.

Camellia was flying here and there, dodging the angry insects, trying to find a solution to end the war.

"Rainbow!" she called the Rainbow Fairy, who was sitting inside a tree hollow, soothing her leg. "Please listen, I have got an idea."

"What idea?" Rainbow asked her, her eyes big with fright.

"I think I know who behind this attack is," Camellia said.

"You do? And who is it?" Rainbow's eyes got even wider.

"Muddy, the Fairy of Swamps," Camellia whispered. "Only she can put a dark spell. And these insects and snakes are under a dark spell, that's why they're so strong and angry."

"Wow, that looks like it," Rainbow said. "Muddy is such an evil fairy. No wonder that she lives so far away, in the swamps. But why would she do that?"

"That is exactly the thing that I'm trying to find out," Camellia said. "Will you come with me?"

"Where?" Rainbow looked at her in astonishment.

"To Swampdirt," Camellia said.

"But why?" Rainbow almost fell down.

"To find her and to ask her to stop the war. We need to know the reason. Maybe it is something that doesn't require a war at all?"

Rainbow looked at her as if she was crazy.

"Camellia, I will never set foot to Swampdirt, are you crazy?"

"But we need to find out…" Camellia asked her.

"No, no, no," Rainbow shook her head. "I'm

already been bitten by one of her snakes. Going to the place which is full of them makes my colorful hair stand on end. You had better go alone, if you want to, or find someone else to go with you."

Camellia realized that it was hopeless. Rainbow was never going to go with her. She was already scared of the war, and further journeys were out of the question for her. Sighing, she left the tree hollow and looked around. She needed to find someone who would be willing to go with her on a journey to Swampdirt.

"There is no other choice for me," she said out loud, full of determination. "I must ask the fairies to stop the war and to come with me to Swampdirt. There is no need to be aggressive. No need at all!"

But all the fairies refused to go with her.

"What are you talking about?" Flow, the Fairy of River said while creating a huge splash to send towards the beetles.

"Shut up and do your magic!" Raya screamed, looking at her angrily.

Other fairies didn't even reply. They were too busy creating magical sparkles and screaming angrily.

Camellia was all alone. She looked around at the war, which had no intention to stop. Finally she decided to go alone.

"Camellia?" two pretty colorful butterflies came

to her, flapping their tiny wings. "Are you going somewhere?"

"Yes, Pinkie, Viol," she said softly to the butterflies, flying towards the edge of the forest. "No one wanted to join me on this journey. But I'm going to go alone. I will prove to everyone that peace is better than war, that calmness and communication is better than aggression. Everybody must understand that."

"I am coming with you!" Pinkie exclaimed.

"Me too!" Viol added, full of determination.

"Oh, thank you so much, my pretty butterflies!" Camellia exclaimed happily. "But the journey is going to be difficult and dangerous, as we are going to Swampdirt. That place is not a good and sunny place. It is dark and scary. Are you sure you want to come with me? You can stay here and wait for me."

"No, no, it is out of the question – I am coming," Pinkie said, and flipped her wings harder, just to prove that she is serious.

"I am also coming!" Viol added. "And don't even try to leave me behind!"

"You are such kind, brave, wonderful butterflies!" Camellia said, smiling. "Well, let's go, then. The sooner we find Muddy and convince her to stop the war, the sooner the war will end and our dance celebration party will take place."

"Dance celebration party?" the butterflies asked.

"Yes, we were going to have a fairy dance celebration party today in the daylight, if only it was peaceful…"

"Don't worry – we shall bring back the peace, together we are strong!" The butterflies said, and Camellia smiled.

## *Chapter 3. Swampdirt*

Sitting down under one of the perched trees, Camellia remembered the attack and got sadder.

"Now that I can't fly, how am I going to get there soon?" She asked the butterflies. "I can only walk, and it will be too late when I get to her."

"Don't worry, Camellia," Pinkie said. "You can walk, and we shall fly by your side. We shall reach there soon, I am sure."

"I hope so," Camellia said, and got up. She brushed the dirt off her pink dress, which had turned brown with the dirt, and started walking. The two butterflies flew alongside her, trying to cheer her up.

They went and went for some time, and it became scarier and scarier. There came no sound at all – not even the sound of singing birds. It was dark, silent, and smelled horribly.

Pinkie and Viol kept looking around them as they flew, fearing that something might spring out on them.

Suddenly Camellia stopped walking and looked around.

"What happened?" Pinkie asked her, stopping, too. Viol hurried to sit on Camellia's shoulder.

"Shh, I think there is someone here," Camellia whispered, putting her finger on her mouth.

"Oh, no!" Viol whispered, trying not to scream.

Something moved in the dried up grass in the dark.

"Snakes!" Camellia shouted and jumped up startled. Viol also jumped up, closing her eyes.

Several dozen snakes were crawling towards Camellia.

"Let's turn back! Go back to our forest!" Viol shouted. "Quick! Hurry up!"

"Turn back? Never!" Camellia said, shaking her head.

"Then what are you going to do? The snakes look angry!" Pinkie said. "They will bite you!"

"And you can't fly!" Viol added, shivering with fright. "You can only walk!"

"You are right, I can't fly," Camellia said. "But I can't return to the forest. By turning back I will not reach my goal. You must know that every problem has its solution."

"Then what is the solution here? To get bitten by the snakes?" Pinkie asked.

"No, of course. I will think of something now," Camellia said. She stood for a minute, until the snakes slithered closer to her, glaring at her angrily. Their eyes were sparkling in the dark, looking like lots of small shiny dots sprinkled on the ground.

After waiting for a few seconds, she started climbing the nearby tree, which was as lifeless and dry as a piece of wood. It was a bit difficult, as she could not use her wings, but in the end she climbed and reached the branches, and started moving from one tree to another by jumping from a branch to a branch. The butterflies flew beside her, shaking their wings hurriedly.

"Oh, Camellia, you are so clever!" Pinkie shouted happily.

Camellia stopped moving from a tree to a tree and looked down. She saw that the snakes had moved to the tree she was on and were trying to reach her by standing on the end of their tails, but as they almost reached her, she jumped to another branch and held on tightly.

After several minutes of trying to catch her, the

snakes got tired of following her and slithered away.

"Wow, that was really scary," Viol said, sitting onto a branch to take a rest.

"But you are so brave, Camellia," Pinkie said, looking at her admiringly. "I don't think I could have made that courageous decision."

"I was also scared, my dear butterflies," Camellia said, smiling, as she sat on a branch. "But I knew that the peace of my forest depended on me and this journey, so I had to take care of that. I had to move forward, and not to return back. I always look ahead of me and go straight where my goal is. Otherwise I will miss my chance to reach my goal."

"What a wonderful piece of advice," Viol exclaimed. "I must remember those words and use them from time to time. I will also teach those words to my friends."

"Exactly," Pinkie said. "Good for you, Camellia. You won the snakes."

"Now I think it is time to move forward until we find Muddy," Camillia said, smiling, as she slowly climbed down the tree. "If only we don't meet any more scary obstacles ahead of us."

"I really hope we won't," Pinkie said.

"The octopus and the snakes were enough for us," Viol added and sat on Camellia's muddy shoulder.

The swamps were all around them. Camellia had to walk very carefully, so that accidentally not to step into one of them. There were toads and frogs sitting here and there on the edges of the swamps or on rocks, croaking loudly.

"Oh, see! Frogs!" Viol said, taken aback. "And toads…"

"Yes, we shall meet more of them here, I think," Camellia said. "It is a strange place, this Swampdirt, isn't it?"

"Looks like that," Pinkie said, flying hurriedly, to keep closer to Camellia.

They continued their way until they reached a big cave that looked like a big black hole in the wall in the dark. Camellia stopped.

"What is that?!" Pinkie whispered.

"I don't know. We have to find out," Camellia said and walked forward.

"I hope there isn't a scary thing there," Viol whispered, shivering from fright.

"But do we really need to see what is inside?" Pinkie asked. "Maybe we can just get past it and move forward?"

"I don't think so," Camellia said, shaking her head slowly. "Whatever is in there will make sure to follow us if we just walk past it. And I want to confront it and not to be followed by it."

"It is getting scarier by each second," Viol whispered.

"Don't be afraid, Viol," Camellia said. "As long as you are with your friends, there is nothing to be afraid of."

"All right," Viol said and took a deep breath.

"Let's keep together," Pinkie said, looking at the big black cave.

Together, they started moving forward towards the cave. Camellia tried to walk as noiselessly as possible. Whatever was in the cave didn't need to be alerted of their arrival.

## *Chapter 4. The Fairy of Swamps*

Camellia and her friends moved noiselessly towards the cave.

"Who has decided that she reserves the right to intrude into my own territory?" Suddenly a screeching voice was heard from the inside.

Camellia and the butterflies gasped and froze in their places, too scared to move forward.

"It is Muddy," Camellia whispered.

The butterflies sat on both of her shoulders, shivering slightly.

"Come inside, let me see you," the voice said.

But Camellia stayed where she was.

"How interesting. You have crossed the borders to come to me, and now that you are here at last, you are scared to move forward?" the Fairy of Swamps thundered from the inside.

Camellia frowned. Muddy seemed to have a point. What was the point of coming all the way here if she was going to be afraid of her? Camellia came one step forward, cleared her throat and said in a voice that was full of determination:

"Hello, Muddy, the Fairy of Swamps. I am Camellia, the Fairy of Flowers."

"Ah, the Fairy of Flowers! Flowers, you said?!" Came the voice, sounding angry. "Of course, flowers, haha, what else? Fairies of Flowers, Rainbows, Sun, Trees, Green Grass, Clouds, Mushrooms... What other wonderful fairies are there in your lovely forest?"

Camellia looked at the butterflies and shrugged.

"Muddy, the Fairy of Swamps, I came because..." she started to say.

"And only I, only I am the Fairy of Swamps! Such a disgusting thing to be the Fairy of," Muddy interrupted her.

"By the way," Camellia said. "Why don't you come out, so that we can communicate normally?"

There was silence. Camellia looked at the butterflies who were staring at the entrance of the cave. Then she heard something moving, and soon they saw Muddy, the Fairy of Swamps.

She looked horrible. Even though she was the

23

same height as Camellia, her entire face and body were covered in dirt, so only her eyes were visible on her face. Her long black hair had stuck together in slim mud. She was wearing a dark and dirty cloth as a dress, which was dripping mud. She glared at Camellia maliciously.

"Oh, you are such a pretty fairy," she said mockingly, walking slowly around Camellia.

Camellia didn't say anything. The butterflies were still sitting on her shoulders, trying not to move.

"So, Camellia, the Fairy of Flowers, tell me, what's the reason that you have started a dangerous journey and have come to my territory tonight?" She asked.

"Well, Muddy," Camellia said, sitting down on a big rock. "A war has started between the Fairyland Forest and the insects. I have suspicions that you are behind the attack."

"And you are correct in your suspicions," Muddy told her, looking very proud of herself. "Of course it was me who started it. Who else?"

"And why, may I know, have you started a war?" Camellia asked her calmly.

"It is none of your business," Muddy snapped, suddenly angry again. "Go back and enjoy your pretty forest."

"I can't," Camellia said. "Unfortunately there is

war at the moment. The pretty forest has turned into debris."

"Oh, poor fairies!" Muddy exclaimed, clapping her dirty hand onto her mouth mockingly. "Too bad, too bad. But what else can you do? Return and live in the debris."

"Please, Muddy, tell me what's the reason of the war," Camellia asked her. "The reason that I am here is to know why you did it."

Muddy laughed. She was very ugly – with her mouth wide open, her teeth blackened and crooked, and she sounded like a crow.

"So you have come in vain, my pretty fairy," she said at last. "Because I am never going to tell you anything."

"Look, Muddy," suddenly Pinkie blurted out. "You had better tell us! We have not come in vain!"

"Yes! And Camellia has lost her powers because of your stupid swamp!" Viol screamed suddenly, and jumped up, startled, amazed at her own courage. "It must not be in vain! She sacrificed her magic to get here!"

"She did?" Muddy looked at Camellia, and she nodded silently. "I have enchanted my swamps, of course, but what surprises me more is how dumb someone can be to decide to take a bath in the swamps, hahaha. How did you manage to touch the swamp, anyways?"

25

"I wasn't planning to take a bath, Muddy," Camellia said, controlling her temper. "I was trying to retrieve my flower that had fallen into it. I touched the swamp surface accidentally."

"How sad. How touching," Muddy said and then turned to look at the butterflies. "And who are you, by the way? Trying to help your little friend, aren't you? I think my spiders will be glad to eat two butterflies for breakfast."

"You will not touch my friends, Muddy," Camellia said angrily. Muddy looked surprised. She had never seen Camellia angry before.

"Oh, only don't tell me you are trying to defend your friends," she said.

"Yes, I am," Camellia said, her eyes sparkling in the dark. "And you will never understand it, because you don't have friends."

For a second Muddy looked like she wanted to say something, but then she got silent and looked at Camellia without saying anything.

## *Chapter 5. Having Friends*

Muddy looked rather sad. Camellia was surprised to see that. She came a few steps closer to Muddy.

"Are you all right?" She asked. She was trying to be as gentle as possible, because she wasn't sure what Muddy wanted.

Muddy shook her head. Camellia frowned. She didn't know if it was a trap or something.

"Camellia, you are right – I don't have friends," Muddy said sadly. Camellia stayed silent and waited.

"Many and many years ago," Muddy said, "when I was the Fairy of Swamps, I thought it was wonderful. The mud, the swamps, and the darkness seemed amazing to me. I was happy and contented to be the Fairy of Swamps. But after all these years I understood that no one surrounded me except the snakes, spiders and scorpions, frogs and toads, octopuses and flies. I realized that I didn't have any friends. Of course I realized it when I was flying and accidentally flew past your forest, clean and bright, sunny and joyful. I hid behind a tree and watched the beautiful fairies playing together, singing, dancing and having fun."

Muddy stopped talking. Camellia didn't know what to say. She could never imagine that Muddy would talk like that.

"And you know what the most awful thing was?" Muddy asked her. Camellia shook her head. "The most awful thing was that no fairy wanted to be friends with me. Yes, they had noticed me," Muddy added hastily. "But they ignored me. They thought they were better than me. But I endured it. I made friends with the insects and snakes that lived with me. I even made friends with the frogs. But they could not be real friends. They had their businesses and didn't want to spend time with me."

Camellia nodded. She was afraid to interrupt Muddy and make her angry again.

"Camellia," Muddy said, "I have never started a war before. But I did last night, because, while I was spying on the forest and the pretty fairies, I learned that today you were going to have a dancing celebration party."

"Oh, yes, we were going to," Camellia said, nodding. "But it most probably will not take place because of the attack," she added sadly.

"That is exactly what I wanted," Muddy said. "I was angry that you had not invited me to the party, and I wanted to disrupt it before it had even started."

Camellia's eyes widened in surprise. So that was the reason of the attack!

"Muddy," she said, "you could just come and tell us that you wanted to participate, too."

"No, no, no, you would never let me participate! Look at me!" Muddy said, shaking her head. As she did so, her dirty hair shook some of the mud off and the mud fell almost on Camellia's feet.

"Oh!" Camellia jumped a step back, accidentally shaking the butterflies off her shoulders. "Muddy, it is important to communicate," she said. "I am sure if you came to me, I would definitely let you participate in our party."

"You would?" Muddy looked at her suspiciously.

"Of course!" Camellia nodded, as if to prove that she was telling the truth.

Suddenly Muddy's eyes got filled with tears. "But I am so ugly, so dirty! Whenever I try to get clean, I get into one of my swamps and get even dirtier! And if I want to wear something different, I stand in my swamp and click my fingers, but my dress becomes even uglier!"

"No, stop it, Muddy! Stop talking, please!" Camellia came forward again. "You are not ugly! And you are dirty because you are... um... covered with dirt! See, now I am also covered with dirt so I am also dirty!"

Muddy looked at Camellia, as if seeing her for the first time. Then she slowly started nodding and smiling. "Yes, exactly. Just look at yourself! There is no pretty Camellia left here," she said and they started to giggle together.

Pinkie and Viol looked at each other and shrugged. It was surprising to see the two fairies giggling together, when only minutes ago one of them was very scary.

## Chapter 6. The Fairy of Fountain

"If you stop the war, you can come to the forest with me," Camellia said excitedly. "And then you can wash in the river and participate in the dance party!"

"Oh, Camellia, thank you very much!" Muddy said. "But I am sure your Fairy of River will never let me wash in her rivers. Also, look at my dress! My hair! My face! And, most importantly, I can't sing or dance."

"Why?" Camellia asked, looking curious.

"Because I sing like a frog and dance like a snake," Muddy explained. "I have learned it from them, see. When I sing and dance like that, all the fairies will either get scared or laugh at me."

"Let me see how you sing and dance, Muddy," Camellia said, smiling. "I will not laugh at you, I promise. And I don't get scared easily, so rest assured."

Muddy nodded. She brought her palms together,

and then started moving them to the sides, at the same time she moved her body from left to right, like a snake, as she stood on the ground. While dancing like a snake, she started to sing, but only croaks came out of her mouth. To make matters worse, her muddy slippery hair sprang up, standing on end, splattering the surroundings with mud.

A piece of mud fell onto Viol, sticking her on the dry tree trunk.

"Ouch!" Viol shouted. Pinkie hurried to help her get rid of the piece of mud and fly back to the fairies again.

"See? I only cause disruption when I sing and dance," Muddy said, seeing that.

"No, no, you were dancing beautifully," Camellia said. "But why did your hair stand on end like that?"

"It is like that every time I sing and dance," Muddy said, laughing.

"Muddy, do you want to be kind?" Camellia asked her suddenly.

Muddy just looked at her and didn't say anything. Camellia raised her eyebrows, waiting for the response.

"I... I don't know what it means," Muddy said at last in a small voice. "What does it mean, to be kind?"

"What? You don't know what it means to be kind? Haven't you ever heard about kindness?" Camellia asked, looking surprised.

Muddy merely shook her head.

"Being kind is the best thing in the world," Camellia started to explain, smiling. "If you want to do good things to others, then you are kind. If you don't want others to suffer, then you are kind. If you want others to be happy and you do everything you can to make them happy, then you are kind. Kindness is the best feeling in the world. When you are kind, you are happy, too, because others surround you with kindness as well."

For a few minutes Muddy was silently looking at Camellia, as if trying to understand the meaning of her words.

"You mean to say that I must do good things instead of bad things if I want to be kind?" She asked slowly.

Camellia nodded.

"And if I'm kind, others will be kind to me, as well?" Muddy continued. Camellia nodded again, this time with a happy smile. She was glad that Muddy was slowly becoming a kind fairy.

"Then, I want to be a kind fairy!" Muddy exclaimed. "I want to be kind, good, happy! I want to make others kind, good and happy, too!" her voice was gradually becoming higher and higher, until she started to yell. "I want to be kind! I want to do kind things!"

Pinkie and Viol gasped. Camellia looked around: the grim darkness of the sky was slowly wearing off. Even Muddy looked around in astonishment. The surroundings were slowly changing. The dark sky turned into a pale blue sky, with the newly risen sun shining high up in the sky.

"What is happening?!" Muddy said, looking up at the sky. "There has never been sunlight here before!"

Then the dry and lifeless trees slowly started to freshen up as small green leaves appeared on the branches. The dark black soil was replaced by thick green grass, which looked like a soft and lush carpet, while the swamps turned into small lakes with crystal clear water. Colorful flowers started to grow in the green grass, filling the surroundings with the most pleasant aroma of roses, violets, lilies and tulips. The air got filled with pleasant trills of the pretty birds that were sitting comfortably on the branches of the trees.

Pinkie and Viol found other colorful butterflies sitting on the flowers and went to make friends with them.

"I can't believe it!" Muddy whispered, looking around the bright, sunny and colorful area that used to be full of disgusting swamps, mud and soil.

Camellia was shining with happiness. She hadn't imagined that kindness could cause such transformation.

34

"If the swamps are gone, what kind of fairy am I now?" Muddy asked Camellia.

"Hmm, let me think… can you click your fingers and make magical sparkle?" She asked Muddy. "I think that way we can understand what fairy you are."

Muddy did as Camellia said: she clicked her fingers to make magical sparkle. Immediately a big fountain burst out of the nearest lake and shot high up to the sky.

"Oh, I think you are the Fairy of Fountains!" Camellia exclaimed. "To be sure, you must go and stand under the fountain. Let's see if it will change your appearance."

"I think you are right," Muddy said and flew towards the center of the small lake, where the fountain was.

"In the meantime, I'll wash in the water and become clean again," Camellia said and entered the lake.

She got instantly clean. Her wings started sparkling again. Camellia was impatient to check her wings if they could work again. And they could! Shouting with happiness, Camellia flew round and round, went to join Pinkie and Viol and showed them her wings.

"This is amazing, Camellia!" the butterflies exclaimed. "It's magical!"

At last Muddy got out from under the fountain and came flying towards Camellia.

Camellia could not recognize Muddy. If she didn't know it was her, she would probably think it was another fairy: Muddy was clean, with white shining face, pretty green eyes and light blond hair. Her long dress was beautiful and light blue, just like the water in the lake, and her long blond hair was shining under the sunlight.

"Muddy, I can't believe this is you!" Camellia exclaimed.

"Me, neither!" Muddy said happily.

"You know, Muddy, I think we must choose another name for you – a more suitable name. Now you are not the Fairy of Swamps, so Muddy isn't appropriate for you. Now you're the Fairy of Fountains. So your name can be Fountain, if you want."

"Of course I want! I am so happy!" Fountain said, happily jumping up and down.

"I think if you come to the dancing party like this, everyone will be pleasantly surprised," Camellia said. "Now, if only to make you a bit more ready for the party," she added, clicking her fingers. Pink sparkle flew out of her hands, went spiraling to Fountain's hair and in a few seconds her hair was made beautifully up, with light blue flowers inside it.

Then Camellia picked up a couple of tulips and

patted Fountain's lips with the petals.

"This will be your lipstick," she said, giggling. "Now I will make you a necklace and then you can look at yourself in the clear mirror of the lake."

She collected small beads and put them in a row onto a thin branch, which she then magically attached onto Fountain's neck.

Fountain could hardly wait to see her new appearance.

"This is amazing!" She exclaimed, seeing her beautiful reflection in the lake.

"Very beautiful," Pinkie and Viol said, smiling at her.

"Let's go to the forest, Fountain!" Camellia said. "I hope the war has ended."

"I'm sure it ended the second I got kind," Fountain said.

The two fairies and the two butterflies started to fly towards the forest. From far they could tell that the war had ended. There were no insects or snakes, and the fairies were creating sparkles to remake their houses magically.

When Camellia and Fountain entered the forest, the other fairies turned to look at them.

"Camellia! The war ended! By the way, who is

this new fairy?" Raya asked.

"This is Fountain, the Fairy of Fountain," Camellia said, smiling. "She will participate in the dance party with us today. She used to be the Fairy of Swamps, but she became kind and everything changed."

The other fairies looked at them with their mouths open.

"Is this Muddy?" Blowie asked. "I can't believe it!"

"Yes, I used to be Muddy. But I understood what it meant to be kind, so I changed," she said. "And my surroundings also changed – now I live in a clean and pleasant area, surrounded by lakes and trees, flowers, birds and butterflies."

Camellia was shining of pride.

"I'm glad that I went on that journey, together with Pinkie and Viol. Otherwise we would never ever know that kindness is the greatest magic of all."

All the other fairies applauded. Fountain also clapped her hands and smiled.

\*\*\*\*

"Girls, if we are going to organize that dance party, we must wear appropriate dresses just like

Fountain!" Rainbow said. "I will make a colorful dress for me."

"And mine will be green," Grassina said hurriedly.

"Mine will be golden, of course," Raya said.

"And mine will be brown, like a chocolate," Willow said.

Camellia looked and smiled, as the fairies wore colorful dresses, made up their hair and got ready for the upcoming dance party that they had been looking forward for such a long time.

But the happiest of them all was Fountain. She knew she had conquered jealousy, maliciousness and aggression. And that was most important of all.

- End -

25507327R00028

Printed in Poland
by Amazon Fulfillment
Poland Sp. z o.o., Wrocław